Hermes and the
Horse with Wings

HEROES IN TRAINING

Hermes and the Horse with Wings

By
Tracey West

Created by
Joan Holub and
Suzanne Williams

Aladdin NEW YORK LONDON TORONTO SYDNEY NEW DELHI

This book is a work of fiction. Any references to historical events, real people, or real places are used fictitiously. Other names, characters, places, and events are products of the authors' imagination, and any resemblance to actual events or places or persons, living or dead, is entirely coincidental.

ALADDIN

An imprint of Simon & Schuster Children's Publishing Division
1230 Avenue of the Americas, New York, NY 10020
First Aladdin paperback edition April 2017
Text copyright © 2017 by Joan Holub and Suzanne Williams
Illustrations copyright © 2017 by Craig Phillips
Also available in an Aladdin hardcover edition.
All rights reserved, including the right of reproduction
in whole or in part in any form.
ALADDIN and related logo are registered trademarks of Simon & Schuster, Inc.
For information about special discounts for bulk purchases,
please contact Simon & Schuster Special Sales
at 1-866-506-1949 or business@simonandschuster.com.
The Simon & Schuster Speakers Bureau can bring authors to your live event.
For more information or to book an event,
contact the Simon & Schuster Speakers Bureau at 1-866-248-3049
or visit our website at www.simonspeakers.com.
Series designed by Karin Paprocki
Cover designed by Karina Granda and Nina Simoneaux
Interior designed by Mike Rosamilia
The text of this book was set in Adobe Garamond Pro.
Manufactured in the United States of America 0317 OFF
2 4 6 8 10 9 7 5 3 1
Library of Congress Control Number 2016960781
ISBN 978-1-4814-8832-7 (hc)
ISBN 978-1-4814-8831-0 (pbk)
ISBN 978-1-4814-8833-4 (eBook)

⚡ Contents ⚡

Greetings,
Mortal Readers,

I am Pythia, the Oracle of Delphi, in Greece. I have the power to see the future. Hear my prophecy:

Ahead, I see dancers lurking. Wait—make that *danger* lurking. (The future can be blurry, especially when my eyeglasses are foggy.)

Anyhoo, beware! Titan giants seek to rule all of Earth's domains—oceans, mountains, forests, and the depths of the Underwear. Oops—make that *Underworld*. Led by King Cronus, they are out to destroy us all!

Yet I foresee hope. A band of rightful rulers called Olympians has begun to form. Though their size and youth are no match for the Titans, they are giant in heart, mind, and spirit. They follow their leader, Zeus, a very special boy. Zeus is destined to become king of the gods and ruler of the heavens.

If he is brave enough.

And if he and his friends work together as one. And if they can learn to use their new amazing flowers—um, amazing *powers*—in time to save the world!

CHAPTER ONE

Four Plus Four

The morning sun shone on four Olympians as they made their way through the countryside of Greece. One of them, a boy named Hades, was walking backward and talking to the others.

"What is a snake's favorite thing to study?" curly-haired Hades asked.

"Um, animal science?" guessed one of the

other Olympians, Athena, a girl with thought-ful gray eyes.

"Nope! Hiss-tory. Get it? *Hissssss*-tory?" Hades repeated, and then he started laughing.

"Ha-ha," replied Hephaestus in a flat voice. The boy walked with the help of a cane carved with skulls and topped with a skull-shaped knob.

The fourth Olympian and the leader of the group, Zeus, frowned. "Hades, I don't mind the jokes, but do they have to be all *snake* jokes?" the black haired, blue-eyed leader complained.

"Sorry, Bro," Hades replied sheepishly. "I know you've got a snake thing. But I guess I've got snakes on my mind, seeing as how we just took down a monster lady with snakes for hair."

Even though Hades and the others looked like mortal boys and girls, they were actually immortal, and their actions were courageous beyond their years. Their biggest mission was to stop their enemies—the giant King Cronus and the king's band of minions, the half-giant Cronies—from taking over the world.

"Excuse me, but I believe *I* took down the monster with snakes for hair," Hephaestus pointed out, waving his cane. "I left her in pieces!"

Athena shook her head. "Oh, really? Because I was the one who tricked her into looking into my aegis so that she turned herself into a stone statue first." She patted the gold shield that she wore on her chest, covered by her cloak. "Beating up a statue is not such a big deal."

Hephaestus's cheeks flushed. "Well, she was a scary statue."

Zeus rolled his eyes as his two friends continued to bicker over who had actually slain the green-haired Medusa.

At least it's better than the snake jokes, he thought.

The four of them were heading back to a village that they had just left the day before. So much had happened in the last twenty-four hours.

Twelve Olympians had started off on another quest given to them by Pythia. She was the Oracle of Delphi, and she could see the future—if not always clearly. (Sometimes her foggy spectacles made it so she couldn't see well, which meant her instructions could be a little confusing!) Pythia had seen that Zeus and the other young Olympians, all of them gods with special powers, would one day overthrow evil King Cronus, who ruled the Terrible Titans.

The twelve Olympians hadn't always been together. Zeus had gone on his first quest with only two others, Poseidon and Hera. On each new quest they fought monsters and other mythical beasts. They found magical items. And they added new Olympians to their group.

All twelve of them had traveled to the village yesterday. Pythia had told them to look for "hairy snakes." Nobody had known exactly what that meant, so the twelve had split up into three groups to try to hunt down the hairy snakes. Now that Zeus's group had succeeded, they were trying to meet back up with the other two groups.

"I think that's the village up ahead," Athena announced. "I wonder if anybody else is back yet? I hope they remembered that this is our meeting place."

"They're probably still out looking for hairy snakes, because they don't exist!" Hephaestus said. "We're the only ones who got it right."

"A monster with snakes for hair," Hades said. "I think it was a good look for her."

Zeus smiled. His brother Hades was also

ruler of the Underworld. He liked creepy things.

"I'm sure the others beat us back here," Zeus said. "At least I hope so."

The village was bustling with people shopping at the market stalls. Hades shook the cloth pouch dangling from his belt, and it made a jingling sound.

"We've still got plenty of gold coins," he said. "I'm going to get some more of that stinky cheese that I got yesterday!"

"Not if you want to hang out with us," came a voice behind them.

Zeus, Hades, Hephaestus, and Athena turned around. Four of their Olympian friends stood there: Hera, Hestia, Demeter, and Poseidon!

The girl speaking was Hera, Zeus's blond-haired, blue-eyed (and sometimes bossy) sister. Hades ran up to her and gave her a hug.

"You guys are back!" he cried.

"Yeah, well, there were no hairy snakes in the mountains," Hera reported.

"Just a lot of goats," Poseidon added.

"Did you find the hairy snakes?" asked Demeter.

"We did," Zeus said, "but it's kind of a long story."

"We want to hear it," Hestia said. "But I think we're all hungry. I'll go make a fire over there, and we can talk while we eat."

Hestia pointed to a meadow just beyond the village.

"I'll help you," Athena offered.

"And I'll help Hades do the shopping, so we don't end up eating a whole bunch of stinky cheese," added Hera.

Hades shook his head. "You have no taste."

It wasn't long before the eight Olympians were gathered around a small fire, started by

Hestia and her magic torch. They roasted sausages on sticks and ate chunks of cheese while Zeus, Hephaestus, Athena, and Hades told their story. They explained how a young thief, Perseus, had led them to Medusa, a monster with snakes for hair—Pythia's "hairy snakes." Athena had tricked Medusa and turned her into a statue.

"So, after my cane destroyed the statue, this horse with wings came flying out of it," Hephaestus said.

"A winged horse? Cool!" said Poseidon.

"Not cool," said Zeus. "He grabbed Bolt and flew away with it!"

Demeter gasped. "No! You have to get Bolt back!"

Bolt was one of Zeus's magical objects. After Zeus had pulled Bolt from a stone at Delphi, he had used Bolt on all of their big quests. The lightning-shaped dagger could grow large or small at Zeus's command. It had saved the Olympians from many monsters—and now it was gone.

Zeus nodded. "The horse flew toward this village. But we can't look for him until we find the others."

"And Pythia might have a new quest for us," Athena reminded him.

Poseidon looked around. "No sign of her yet?"

"She might be waiting until all twelve of us are together again," Hera guessed.

"We've got four and four, but we need four more," Hades quipped.

Zeus looked back at the village. "I don't see anyone here yet from our group. Maybe we should ask if anyone has seen them."

Then Hestia pointed to Zeus. "Look! Chip is glowing!"

Zeus looked down at the smooth oval stone that he wore around his neck. Chip was his second magical object and helped guide the Olympians in the right direction. Right now a big red *C* was glowing on the stone.

"That's new," Hera remarked.

"Chip's trying to tell us something," Athena said. "Do you think the *C* stands for 'Cronies'?"

Suddenly the group heard a commotion in the distance.

"Uh, yeah, Bro. . . . I think that *C* definitely stands for 'Cronies,'" Hades said, staring past Zeus. His pale face was even paler than usual as he pointed a shaking finger toward the village.

Zeus looked up from Chip. He could hear screaming. Out of nowhere, three hulking half-giants, soldiers of King Cronus, stomped through the market.

Zeus reached for Bolt around his waist out of habit—but of course it wasn't there. "Quick! Put out our fire!" he yelled.

Poseidon jabbed his magical object—a three-pronged trident—into the dirt. Water sprung from the ground. Poseidon pointed the trident at the fire, and water doused the flames.

But it was too late—the Cronies had seen them. They charged toward the Olympians.

"Cane, stop them!" Hephaestus yelled, waving his cane in front of him. But the cane didn't do a thing. "Come on, cane!" Hephaestus cried angrily.

Zeus did a quick check of the magical objects they had. Hades's Helm of Darkness—a helmet that made him invisible, Demeter's magic seeds, Hera's future-telling peacock feather, and Athena's Thread of Cleverness wouldn't help them fight the Cronies.

But maybe . . .

"Athena, use the aegis to turn them to stone!" Zeus yelled.

Athena reached for her cloak and was about to pull it away to reveal the magic shield underneath. Then she stopped.

"But . . . they're people. Sort of. They're not monsters," she said. "I don't think I can do it."

The three Cronies were almost on them. One carried a heavy club. One carried a sword. The third carried a club with spikes all over it.

"Well, look who we found," yelled one of the Cronies. "A bunch of puny Olympians! Let's squash them like ants!"

Chapter Two

A Messenger Arrives

"Guys, I think this is the part where we run!" Hades yelled.

"I got this!" Poseidon exclaimed.

He aimed his trident at the three Cronies. A powerful wave of water shot from the weapon.

Bam! Bam! Bam! It knocked down the Cronies one by one.

"Now we run!" Zeus yelled.

The eight Olympians raced away from the

village. Zeus looked back over his shoulder. The Cronies were out cold. But they'd soon be back on the Olympians' tail.

"Chip, which is the safest way to go?" Zeus asked his magical amulet.

"Hat-tip ay-wip!"

Chip had its own special language, Chip Latin. It was kind of like Pig Latin, only you moved the first letter of each word to the end of the word and added "ip."

A black arrow glowed on Chip to show which way he meant.

"To the orchard!" Zeus yelled.

The eight Olympians dashed to the apple orchard at the edge of the meadow. Then they ran through the rows of trees until they emerged on the other side.

"Eep-kip oing-gip!" Chip told Zeus.

"Don't stop!" Zeus yelled. "Keep going straight."

Hephaestus, who had been a little behind everyone else, stopped and put his hands on his knees. "You know, all this running isn't so easy for me," he said.

Zeus nodded. He knew that as a young boy Hephaestus had been in a shipwreck that had hurt his leg. That was why Hephaestus used the cane.

Hades jogged back to them. He held out his metal helmet. "Here, use this," he suggested. "That way, if you fall behind, you'll be invisible."

Hephaestus smiled and took it from him.

"Nice teeth," Hades joked. "Didn't know you could smile like that."

Hephaestus put on the helmet, and disappeared.

"I'll catch up!" he promised.

The Olympians kept moving. They traveled over hills and through a wheat field, until they came to the edge of a thick forest.

"Afe-sip," Chip said.

"We can stop now!" Zeus announced.

They all fell to the grass, sweaty and tired. After a few minutes Poseidon raised himself up and tapped his trident on the ground once more. A tiny spring bubbled up.

"So thirsty," he said, taking a big drink.

"That was a pretty nice water blast you came up with back there, Bro," Hades praised him.

"I got lucky," Poseidon said. "There was an underground spring right beneath us in that meadow. I just tapped into it."

Hera took a peacock feather from the pocket of her tunic.

"Feather, please don't make a fuss, but see if the Cronies are still chasing us," she commanded.

Her feather, which only obeyed her when she spoke in rhyme, flew away.

Zeus turned to Athena. "What happened back there? Why didn't you turn those Cronies into stone?"

Her gray eyes looked down toward the shield, hidden beneath her cloak. "Remember on Medusa's island, when we saw all those people she had turned to statues?" she asked, shuddering at the memory. "I don't want to do that to people. Not even Cronies."

Zeus nodded. "I see what you mean. I guess I'm so used to fighting now that I don't always think about *who* we're fighting."

At that moment a cane came floating up to them—a cane with an invisible Hephaestus attached to it. He took off the helmet and appeared before them.

"That was a close one!" he said. "It's a good thing I—hey!"

Hera's peacock feather brushed against his

face as it flew back to her. She held it in front of her and looked into the feather's colorful eye.

"See any Cronies?" Zeus asked.

Hera raised an eyebrow. "No," she replied, "but it looks like there's another kid coming toward us."

"Anyone we know?" Poseidon asked hopefully, but Hera shook her head.

"Hestia, Poseidon, have your magical objects ready," Zeus commanded.

"What about my cane?" Hephaestus asked.

"Uh, you need to learn how to work that thing first," Hera snipped. The boy frowned, but he stood next to the rest of the group, cane down.

The tall wheat in the field next to them began to rustle, and then a boy stepped out. He was about the same age as the rest of them, ten years old, but he was skinnier than any of them. He had dark hair, and his bright blue eyes looked weary with exhaustion as he flopped down next to the group.

"Finally!" he said, clearly winded. "You guys are not easy to find. I had to take a boat, and a cart, and another boat, and then walk. I hate walking!"

"Who are you, and why were you trying to find us?" Zeus asked suspiciously.

"I'm Hermes," he said. "And I have a message for you from Pythia!"

CHAPTER THREE
The Flying Boy

The Olympians gasped.

"How do you know Pythia?" Zeus asked. He had never seen her speak to anyone else but the group of Olympians.

"I don't—I mean, I didn't until a few days ago," Hermes replied. "I was flying past her at Delphi, and she—"

Hera interrupted him. "Wait, did you say 'flying'?"

"That's what I said," the boy answered.

Hera snorted and turned to Zeus. "He's obviously making all of this up. Do you see any wings on him?"

Hermes rolled his eyes. "Do you guys want this message or not? Of course I don't have wings. I'm not some Harpy," he said, annoyed. "I use my winged sandals to fly. Or at least I used to, until some jerk stole them from me."

Athena's eyes narrowed. "You mean those winged sandals, the ones that Zeus is carrying?" she asked, pointing to the sandals hanging from Zeus's belt.

"Hey! Where did you get those?" Hermes exclaimed. "Listen, I'll make you a deal. I'll give you the message from Pythia, but only if you give me back my sandals."

Athena looked at Zeus. "Hera could be right. This might be a trick to get those sandals from you."

But Zeus remembered something. Perseus, the boy who had given Zeus the sandals, had said they had been stolen from an Olympian.

"Are you an Olympian?" Zeus asked.

Hermes shrugged. "That's what the lady with the glasses said. And then she started babbling about destiny and 'overgrowing the tight ones,' or something like that. She kept saying the future was foggy." Zeus noticed that Hermes talked really fast.

"That sounds like Pythia, all right," Hades piped up.

"Yeah, it sounds like she meant that Hermes is supposed to join us so we can overthrow the Titans—not overgrow the tight ones," added Poseidon.

"Whatever," said Hermes. "Just please give me my sandals back, and I'll give you the message."

Zeus untied the sandals from his belt and held them out.

"Boltbrain, what are you doing?" Hera snapped. Her blue eyes flashed with alarm.

"I believe him," Zeus replied. "Besides, we'll know if he's lying once he puts them on."

Hermes's eyes lit up as he took the sandals from Zeus. He strapped them onto his bare feet.

"Woo-hoo!" he cried. To the amazement of the other Olympians, Hermes began to lift right off the ground!

"See? I told you!" Hermes crowed, a big grin on his face.

"Okay, okay, you got your sandals. Now what's the message?" Hera demanded.

Hermes didn't answer. He was too busy having fun! He zipped up into the air and then flew in a loop above them.

"Wheeeeeeeeee!"

Hera folded her arms. "Well, now he's just showing off."

"Hermes! What's the message?" Zeus yelled up to him.

The boy zipped back down and hovered in front of Zeus, his feet not touching the ground.

"Find the force that sings," Hermes reported, and then he flew straight up again.

"The force that sings?" Hades asked.

"That's what she said," Hermes called down as he swooped across the sky above them. "I told her it didn't make sense, but she said you would figure it out."

Athena started to whisper the message over and over. "Force that sings . . . force that sings . . ."

Hermes hovered in front of Zeus again. "Well, nice meeting you guys. See ya. Got things to do. Places to go." Then he started to fly away.

"Wait!" Zeus yelled. "Don't go!"

Hermes stopped and looked back. "Why not?"

"Because Pythia was right—you're an Olympian," Zeus said. "The fact that the flying sandals work for you proves it. They are your magical object, just like the magical objects we all have." Zeus gestured toward the other Olympians and their objects. It made Zeus miss Bolt even more. "That means you're one of us. We're all gods," Zeus explained.

"And we're destined to take down King Cronus and the Titans," Poseidon chimed in.

"You mean that King Cronus over there?" Hermes asked, pointing into the woods.

The Olympians spun around, ready to fight—and saw nothing but trees. Behind them Hermes was laughing.

"Made you look!" he said, doubled over.

"That wasn't funny," Hephaestus grumbled, slamming his cane into the ground.

Hermes laughed again. "I'll tell you what's funny. Thinking that a bunch of kids like us could take down King Cronus."

"We're not just kids. We're Olympians," Hera told him. "And it's going to take all of us to do it, so even though I hate to admit it, we need you, Fly Guy."

Hermes flew over to her. "Fly Guy? Not bad. Listen, I'm no fan of King Cronus, but if you really think we can defeat him because of destiny, then you're nuttier than that almond tree over there."

Zeus was getting angry now. Who did this Hermes person think he was, anyway?

"You think we can't do it? We've already defeated Titans, like Typhon."

Hermes raised an eyebrow. "That windbag?"

"And Hyperion. That dude could throw a mean fireball," Poseidon remembered.

"And we've battled lots of monsters," added Hestia. "Like the Stymphalian birds."

Hermes looked impressed. "That was you guys?"

"Yes," answered Zeus. "And the more Olympians we meet, the stronger we get."

"Please come with us," said Demeter sweetly. "Just go on one quest with us, and you'll see what we mean."

"You mean the quest to find the force that sings?" Hermes asked. "That just sounds plain silly."

Athena piped up, "I think she means the horse with wings. The horse that stole Zeus's Bolt."

Hermes looked intrigued. "A horse with wings? Now, that sounds interesting. I'll go. But if we're going to do this, we should get started. Let's move it!"

He began to fly off.

"Wait! I need to ask Chip which way to go," Zeus said.

"Who's Chip?" Hermes said, flying back to them.

Zeus touched Chip. "Chip helps us get where we need to go. Chip, which way to the horse with wings?"

A black, glowing arrow appeared on Chip.

"To the west!" Zeus cried.

CHAPTER FOUR

A Magic Wand

They marched along. Hermes flew ahead, quickly becoming a dot in the sky ahead of them.

"He looks like some kind of bird," Hestia mused.

The shape in the sky got bigger as Hermes flew back toward them. He stopped and hovered in the air.

"Can't you guys go any faster?" he complained.

"Sorry. We don't all have winged sandals, you know," Hera huffed as she hurried along.

"Yeah, but you're Olympians, right? Don't you have some magical way to get around? Or do you have to walk everywhere?" he asked, flying alongside them.

"Our powers don't work like that," Zeus said. "We each have powers connected to our magical objects. Like you and your sandals."

Hermes nodded. "I have a magic wand, too."

Hermes reached behind his back and produced an unusual-looking staff. It was gold, with two snakes wrapped around the base and two wings at the very top.

"Where'd that come from?" Hades asked.

"I told you, it's a *magic* wand," Hermes replied.

Hera put her hands on her hips. "So what does it do?"

"Lots of things," Hermes said, shrugging.

"Like what?" Hera asked. "Show us."

"Are you kidding? This is a super-special important magical wand. I don't do tricks with it, like someone in a traveling show," he said.

Hera shook her head. "Just as I thought. It's not really magic."

"Think what you want," said Hermes, and then he started whistling as he flew ahead of them.

"Hey, find us a place to camp!" Zeus called after him. "It's going to be dark soon."

"Will do!" Hermes called behind him.

Poseidon walked up next to Zeus. "Do you really trust that dude, Bro?"

"I'm not sure yet, but he's got a good view from up there," Zeus replied. "And we need to set up camp soon."

"My feather could have found us a good spot," Hera pointed out.

Zeus sighed. "Listen, we need him to stick with us. He is annoying, but he could help us out."

Hermes zipped back in front of them. "I found a great place to camp up ahead. Follow me!"

Hermes flew low to the ground as the others followed him. They walked over a small hill and down into a valley on the other side. Hermes flew to a creek and stopped.

"Not bad, right?" he asked.

The others caught up to him.

"It's pretty nice," Hera admitted. Hermes nodded to a fallen log. "It even comes with a place to sit."

He did a little bow and waved his hand. "After you, my lady."

Hera rolled her eyes but sat down on the log, tired after walking all day. Demeter and Hades joined her.

"I'll start a fire," Hestia offered.

Hera reached for her pack. "I've still got some chee—ow!"

Hera jumped up from the log, frantically brushing off her arms and legs. It looked like she was doing a funny little dance—but she didn't look too happy about it!

"Ants!" she yelled. "They're all over me!"

Hades and Demeter jumped up too.

"There's so many of them!" Hades wailed.

Zeus looked over at Hermes, who was laughing. "Ha! You got ants in your pants!" Hermes said.

Hera's face was bright red. "You mean you did this on purpose?"

"Just trying to lighten the mood," replied Hermes. "You guys are so serious, with all this stuff about battling Titans."

Hades brushed ants off his arm. "I like jokes, but not ones that make me itch!"

Zeus turned to Hermes. "I know you're just

trying to be funny, but we have a good reason to be serious. King Cronus is totally evil. If we stand any chance of taking him down, we've got to stick together."

Hermes nodded. "You're right," he said. He held out his hand. "Let's shake on it."

Zeus reached out to shake Hermes's hand. He felt something wriggling in his palm, and jumped back with a shout. A tiny garden snake fell to the ground and wiggled away.

"Gotcha again!" Hermes said, grinning.

"Hey!" Zeus cried. "Why'd you do that?" Zeus's heart was pounding. He hated snakes—even little ones!

"Come on," Hermes said. "Admit it. That was pretty funny."

Zeus was not about to admit anything. "Let's find another camping spot," he said. He turned and walked away from the creek.

Hermes landed and walked next to him. "Man, you guys really are no fun. I don't know if I'll be able to hang out with you for much longer if it's going to be like this."

Zeus didn't answer. He just kept walking. He felt like telling Hermes to just fly away, but he couldn't. He had to keep the Olympians together—even the annoying ones.

Hera, on the other hand, did not have Zeus's patience.

"You know, Hermes, if you don't like it, you can—"

"Hera, stay out of it," Zeus snapped. "We all need to—aaaahhhhh!"

"Zeus!" Athena cried.

The ground had suddenly disappeared beneath his feet!

CHAPTER FIVE

Bears ... or Birds?

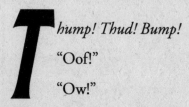

Thump! Thud! Bump!

"Oof!"

"Ow!"

"Hey!"

Zeus and the other Olympians fell through a hole in the ground. They slid down a steep, slippery dirt slope and landed at the bottom of a pit.

Zeus sat up, stunned. "Is everyone okay?" he asked.

Everyone except Hermes, who managed to fly above the hole, had fallen with him—Hades, Poseidon, Hephaestus, Hera, Demeter, Hestia, and Athena. Some of the Olympians had landed on top of one another.

"Get your elbow out of my eye!" Hephaestus complained to Poseidon.

"Get your foot out of my ear!" Poseidon shot back. "It stinks!"

"I'm all right," Hera said, getting to her feet. "But what just happened?"

Zeus looked around. They appeared to be in a pit that had been dug out of the ground. A huge mat of grass had fallen into the pit with them.

Athena spoke up. "It looks like a trap. Someone dug the hole and put the grass mat on top so that whoever walked onto the mat would fall inside."

 41

"Who would do something like that?" Hades asked.

Grrrrrrrrrrrrr.

The Olympians tensed.

"Did you hear that?" Demeter asked in a whisper.

GRRRRRRRRR!

Everyone looked up to see two creatures looking into the pit. They looked like bears, with brown, furry faces and mouths full of sharp teeth.

"They kind of look furry and cute," Demeter remarked.

"Cute? Do you see those teeth?" Hephaestus shot back.

Then the bear creatures started to talk.

"Look at that, Brrrotherrr!" said one.

"I see. So many tasty trrreats!" said the other. They both laughed.

"I think I've heard of these guys," Hades

whispered. "They're half human, half bear—and all bad!"

"What do you want with us?" Hera yelled up to them.

The two bear men laughed. "Why, we want you for dinnerrr, of courrrse!"

"Good luck trying!" Hera shot back. "We're not some mere mortals, you know. We're Olympians!"

"Sounds delicious!" said one bear, and then he turned to his brother. "Come on. Let's go starrrt a nice firrre!"

The two bear men turned and lumbered away.

Zeus turned to the others. "Okay, they don't seem too bright. Athena, let's use your Thread of Cleverness to get out of here. We need to move quickly."

"Let me handle this!" Hermes said.

The wings on his sandals began to flap, and Hermes flew up and out of the pit.

"Figures that Birdbrain would ditch us," Hera remarked.

Zeus wasn't sure what to think. Hermes had said he would handle things, but could they trust him?

Beside Zeus, Athena was already working quickly. She had placed a stick in front of her. With her magic Thread of Cleverness she spelled out a word: "ladder."

In a flash, the stick transformed into a ladder that reached all the way to the top of the pit. Zeus held the bottom to steady it.

"Okay, one at a time!" he said. "When you get out, run back toward the creek."

The Olympians scrambled up the ladder one by one until only Hephaestus and Zeus were left. Zeus supported Hephaestus from behind as the boy climbed up the ladder. Then Zeus climbed out of the pit last.

He expected to break into a run to catch up to his friends—but instead he found everyone gathered around Hermes. The boy had a little brown bird perched on top of each hand. The birds were squawking and flapping around.

"Come on. We have to get out of here before the bear guys come back!" Zeus cried.

"We don't have to," Demeter said. "Hermes turned them into birds!"

Hermes held up his hands. "The only dinner they'll be eating tonight is worms."

Zeus was confused. "How did you do that?" he asked.

"With my magic wand, of course," Hermes replied.

"Well, we didn't actually see him," said Hera. "For all I know, he could be lying. Those could just be ordinary birds."

"I'm not lying!" Hermes protested. "I flew

out and zapped the bears with my magic wand before they knew what was happening. Then, *bam*! They were birds."

"I think he's telling the truth, Bro," said Hades.

Zeus frowned. He didn't know what to believe. He touched Chip.

"Chip, can you show us a safe way to the horse with wings?" he asked.

"Es-yip!" Chip replied. Then a green glowing arrow appeared on its surface.

"We might as well keep going, then," Zeus decided.

Hermes waved his hands, and the two birds flew off. Then he lifted up into the air.

"I'll go find us a campsite!" he said, and zipped ahead of them.

"No ants this time, Birdbrain!" Hera yelled after him.

CHAPTER SIX

Ron for Short

They found another campsite and settled in for the night. Zeus was too worried about the bears returning to get a good night's sleep. But he didn't hear a single growl that night, just the hoot of an owl. He finally drifted off when the sun was just starting to rise.

He woke up to find Poseidon shaking him. "Rise and shine, Bro! We've got a flying horse to find!"

Zeus sat up and rubbed his eyes. "Yeah, sure," he said with a yawn.

Hera marched up to him. "Well, if it isn't our lazy leader," she said. "We've all been up for an hour already."

Zeus almost started to argue that he had been up all night on guard, but he knew it was no use arguing with Hera.

"I'm up," he said grumpily.

Demeter walked over and handed him a hunk of bread and an apple. "Here, have some breakfast," she said with a smile.

"Thanks," Zeus said, taking a bite of the fruit. The juice dripped down his chin, and he wiped it with his sleeve.

"I already sent my feather scouting ahead," Hera reported. "There's a kingdom not too far from here. I bet that's where we'll find the horse with wings."

Zeus realized that he might be close to finding Bolt again, and he instantly felt more awake. He missed having his magical object by his side. "Awesome! Is everybody ready to go?"

"Yes," Hera replied. "And guess what? Fly Guy is still hanging around."

Zeus followed her gaze and saw Hermes and Hades laughing about something.

That's good, he thought. *If he likes us, he'll stick with us.*

"Let's pack up and head for the kingdom, then!" Zeus called out.

They followed Chip down a dusty road. After they walked for about an hour, they found themselves looking down on a small, sprawling kingdom.

"Fancy," Hades remarked. "Anybody know where we are?"

"No idea," said Zeus. "But I guess we'll find out."

"I think I see a fountain in there," Poseidon said, pointing. "Boy, am I thirsty. Can we stop and get a drink?"

"I don't see why not," Zeus said. "And then we can ask if anyone's seen a flying horse."

They followed the road into a busy village center. Water bubbled up from a round stone fountain, and the Olympians ran toward it.

"Sweet, sweet water!" Poseidon cried.

Zeus walked up and bent down to get a drink. But as he tilted his head for a sip, he felt a hand on his back, and then found himself falling forward into the water!

Zeus quickly climbed out of the fountain, damp and sputtering. Hermes was right in front of him, laughing.

"Did you have a nice bath?" Hermes asked.

"That was *not* funny!" Zeus said, shaking the water out of his hair. "You know, if you can't—"

"Zeus!" Hera had called his name. He turned to see her pointing to a white horse right next to them—a white horse with wings.

"We found it!" Zeus cried. Forgetting to be angry with Hermes, he ran to the horse. The other Olympians followed him.

The horse was drinking from the fountain. A boy held on to the horse's reins. The boy had curly blond hair that grew down to his shoulders. He looked to be about as old as the Olympians, but he was short for his age.

But that wasn't what interested Zeus. He saw Bolt hanging from the boy's belt like a dagger!

"Who are you?" Zeus demanded.

"I'm Bellepheron, but you can call me 'Ron' for short," the boy replied. "Everyone does."

"And Ron sure *is* short," Hades whispered to Poseidon, who giggled.

"So, Ron, I think there's been a mistake here,"

Zeus said. "You see, this flying horse stole my dagger, and now it looks like you have it."

"This thing is yours?" Ron asked, looking down at it. Then he looked up at Zeus. "So who are you, anyway?"

"I'm Zeus," Zeus replied. "And I'd like my dagger back, please."

Ron bit his lower lip. He didn't answer right away.

"Well, I don't think I can do that," Ron said, his voice shaking nervously. "I'm going to need it."

"Sorry, but *I* need it," Zeus said. "So please give it back."

Ron shook his head. "I guess . . . I guess you'll have to fight me for it."

"I don't have to do that," Zeus told him. Then he yelled out, "Bolt! Return!"

CHAPTER SEVEN

A Monstrous Tale

At Zeus's command, Bolt flew out of Ron's belt and returned to Zeus's hand. It felt so good to have Bolt back!

How dare that kid try to keep Bolt! Zeus thought. *He looks like a scaredy-cat anyway. I'll give him something to be scared of. . . .*

"Bolt, large!" Zeus yelled.

Ron's eyes got wide as Bolt instantly grew into a lightning bolt as big as Zeus.

"I'm sorry!" Ron cried, holding his hands up in front of him. "I wasn't trying to steal your lightning thing. It's just . . . I don't know what to do."

He started to cry, and the white horse nuzzled his face.

Hera stomped up. "Nice going, Boltbrain!" she scolded Zeus. "You made the kid cry."

"He had Bolt, and he wasn't going to give it back!" Zeus protested.

Hera put an arm around Ron. "Why don't you come with us? We'll find somewhere quiet, and you can tell us what's wrong."

Ron nodded and sniffled, wiping away his tears.

Hera led the boy away from the busy village center. The winged horse—and the other Olympians—followed them. They all stopped under the shade of a tall tree.

"Thanks for being nice to me," Ron said.

"Yeah, she's nicer to you than she is to any of us," Hades chimed in.

"That's because Zeus needs to pick on someone his own size," Hera said, glaring at Zeus.

"He had Bolt!" Zeus protested. "Besides, he's short, but he's no little kid. He's our age."

Ron was stroking the horse's mane.

"Is that your horse?" Hestia asked him.

"It can't be," Hephaestus argued. "That horse sprang to life when I destroyed the statue of Medusa."

"I only met him yesterday," Ron answered. "I was sitting outside the castle, and he flew down from the sky and landed in front of me. At first I was scared, but he walked right up to me. So I fed him some hay from the royal stables, and he's been hanging around me ever since."

"Aw, that's such a nice story!" said Demeter. "He's a beautiful horse."

"I know," Ron said. "He's my friend. I named him Pegasus."

The horse whinnied, as if he approved of the name.

"So why do you need Bolt, anyway?" Zeus asked.

Ron sighed. "To fight the Chimera."

"Kie-meer-uh?" Athena repeated.

Ron nodded. "It's a terrible monster that lives just outside the kingdom. It's part lion, part goat, and part snake."

Zeus shuddered. "Which part is the snake?"

"I'm not sure, exactly," Ron replied. "What I know is that the Chimera only comes out at night and tries to eat the people in the countryside. They're terrified of it, and they've been asking my uncle, King Iobates, to do something about it."

"So, did he?" Zeus asked.

"He sent out his best soldiers, but they returned to the castle babbling and shaking with fear," said Ron. "Uncle Iobates wasn't sure what to do. Then yesterday he saw me with Pegasus."

Ron stopped and looked up at Pegasus sadly. "He said, since I had a fancy horse that can fly, that the gods must have decided I was some kind of hero. He said I should prove myself to him by slaying the Chimera. That's why I needed Bolt. I have to kill the monster."

"But you're just a kid!" Poseidon said. "I mean, we are too, but we have powers and stuff, being Olympians and all."

At Poseidon's comment, Ron's eyes widened. "You're the *Olympians*? The ones they've been telling stories about? Then you guys can help me!"

Hephaestus snorted. "No, thanks! We've got enough monsters to deal with on our own."

"Hephaestus!" Hera exclaimed. "This is what we do."

Hermes started to fly in a circle around the group. "I thought Pythia said to find the flying horse. We found it. Aren't we done here?"

"But don't you see? This is *why* we were supposed to find the flying horse," Zeus said. "It's not just about getting Bolt back. We need to help Ron stop this Chimera. Hera was right—it's what we do."

"You can say that again, Bro!" said Poseidon.

"Yeah, we've faced a lot worse," Hades said. "How bad could a part-lion, part-goat, part-snake be?"

"It all depends on where the parts are," Poseidon reckoned. "I mean, if it has the head of a goat and the tail of a lion, not too bad."

"From the stories people tell, it's pretty bad," Ron said. "Although, most people don't live to tell the stories."

The Olympians were quiet for a second. Then Hera piped up.

"It doesn't matter," she said. "We'll still help you."

"Right!" said Demeter and Hestia.

Zeus looked at Hephaestus. He was scratching lines in the dirt with his cane. He caught Zeus looking at him and sighed. "Fine. Let's fight this thing."

"We might as well," Hermes said, still flying in circles. "It'll be more interesting than hanging around under this tree all day."

"Let's go to my uncle's castle," Ron suggested. "We can get weapons there."

"We've each got our own weapons," Zeus said.

"Not all of us," Hera reminded him. "I mean, my

feather is awesome, and so are Demeter's seeds, but when it comes to fighting. we've been using rocks and sticks. I wouldn't mind a nice shiny sword."

"Uncle Iobates has plenty!" Ron said. "And I'm sure he'll be impressed that you're Olympians and give you as many as you want."

"Let's just get going so we can get this over with!" Hermes called down, flying above them.

The Olympians followed Ron, who led them, with the flying horse walking next to him.

"Why are you walking when you have a flying horse?" Hermes asked.

"Well, I, um, don't want to tire him out," Ron said.

"Look at him! He's strong! Come on. Hop on and join me up here!" Hermes urged. The wings on his shoes fluttered as he flew in loops overhead.

"Yeah, well, maybe later," Ron replied, looking nervous.

Hephaestus looked at him. "What, are you afraid or something?"

Ron's face turned red. "Uh, yeah. I've always been afraid of heights!"

Hephaestus shook his head. "What would you have done if we hadn't shown up?" he wondered. "You're lucky we found you."

Ron nodded. "Believe me, I know."

They started up a hill crowned by a stone palace. Hermes flew ahead of them. A few minutes later he circled back.

"You guys might want to take cover," he said. "It looks like rain."

Zeus looked up. The sun was shining in the blue sky, and there wasn't a cloud in sight.

"What do you—*ahhhhhh!*"

Zeus screamed as six small, wriggling garden snakes rained down onto his head. He pushed them away and ran, his heart pounding. When he felt safe, he stopped and looked up. Hermes was hovering above him, laughing.

"Oh, man, that was classic!" Hermes said. "You should have seen your face!"

Anger bubbled up inside Zeus. "That is IT!" he thundered. "I am sick and tired of your stupid pranks. If you don't want to be with us, then just leave! Get out of here!"

Hermes looked startled. "Come on. It was just a joke."

"Being an Olympian is not a joke!" Zeus thundered, and for a second he thought he could feel the ground rumble underneath his feet.

"Fine!" Hermes shot back, and then he zipped away, back toward the village.

Zeus watched him go, his heart still pounding. When he turned around, he saw the other Olympians staring at him. They looked shocked—and a little scared.

"Bro, are you okay?" Poseidon asked.

"I'm fine," Zeus answered.

"Well, you don't *seem* fine," Hera said. "You totally freaked out! I mean, Hermes is annoying, but not half as annoying as Hephaestus, and you've never freaked out on him."

"Hey!" Hephaestus protested.

It was the snakes, Zeus thought. Hermes even had snakes on that "magic wand" that he carried. It was like Hermes knew Zeus's exact weakness and had focused on it. But Zeus didn't say that.

"We don't need him anyway," Zeus said instead, and continued to march up the hill. "There are still eight of us, plus Ron, and this is just one monster."

The Olympians exchanged worried glances. But there was nothing to do now. Hermes was gone.

"Come on," said Poseidon, trying to lighten the mood. "Let's go get some cool swords!"

CHAPTER EIGHT

Ambush!

When they arrived at the palace, two guards greeted them. One of them took Pegasus from Ron. The other led Ron and the eight Olympians to the weapons hold inside the castle. A stern-looking man wearing a crown was waiting for them with a frown on his face.

"What is all this about, Bellepheron?" he asked. "I charged you with slaying the

Chimera—you and your fine flying horse. What are you doing with this group of ragged-looking children?"

"Hey, who are you calling ragged-looking?" Hera asked.

"Well, Sis, it *has* been a long time since any of us had a bath," Poseidon pointed out.

"Such rudeness! Guards, remove them!" King Iobates ordered.

"Uncle, no!" Ron protested. "These aren't ordinary children. They're Olympians, and they're going to help me!"

A spark flickered in the king's dark eyes. "Olympians, you say? These messy munchkins?" He laughed. "Nephew, you have been fooled!"

Hades stepped forward. He slipped on his helmet and turned invisible immediately.

"Could an ordinary kid do this?" he asked, his voice coming out of his invisible body.

"Or this?" Hestia asked. She held up her torch, and a flame started to flicker.

King Iobates looked impressed. "Very well, then. Perhaps I was mistaken. And you intend to help us rid the kingdom of the monster?"

Zeus nodded. "Yes, sir."

The king looked distracted. "Hmm, very interesting," he said. "Take what weapons you wish. I must go. Do not fail me, Nephew!"

"I won't, Uncle!" Ron promised as the king hurried off.

Poseidon walked into the center of the room and whistled. "Flipping fish sticks! Look at all this gear!"

Zeus gazed around the weapons hold for the first time. Swords, staffs, and spears hung from every wall.

Hephaestus sniffed. "I could make stuff better than this in my sleep," he said.

Zeus couldn't argue with him. Hephaestus was a master metalworker. But the king's weapons were nothing to sneeze at.

Hera took a sword off the wall. "Check it out!" she said, waving the sword in front of her. Poseidon jumped out of the way.

"Are you sure you know how to use that thing?" he asked.

"I can learn," Hera promised.

"I think I'll stick with my aegis and my Thread of Cleverness," Athena said. "I won't feel bad turning a dangerous monster to stone."

"And I'll stick with my torch," said Hestia.

Demeter picked up a spear topped with a sharp point. "This is kind of cool," she said.

Hades picked up a club with spikes coming out of it. "Wicked!" he said with a grin.

Zeus had Bolt, Hephaestus had his cane, and Poseidon had his trident. The only one who

 71

hadn't decided on a weapon was Ron. He stared at the walls, his eyes wide.

"Have you ever trained with any of these?" Zeus asked him.

Ron shook his head. "My mom only sent me to live with Uncle Iobates a few months ago. She thought it would help me get over my fears."

"Like your fear of heights?" Zeus wanted to know.

"Yes," Ron replied. "And the dark. And thunderstorms. And water. And snakes. And . . ."

"I think I understand," Zeus said. "About the snakes, anyway."

"Well, I'm still afraid of *all* those things," Ron said, and then he sighed. "And now I have to go face a monster."

Ron looked really scared. What kind of uncle would send a regular kid out all by himself to face a monster? Not a nice one, Zeus guessed.

Then Zeus saw a glow coming from Chip. An arrow was pointing at the swords on the wall.

"I think Chip has an idea," Zeus said. He walked toward the wall of swords. The arrow pointed right at a sword with a gleaming white handle.

"His-tip ne-oip or-fip on-Rip!" Chip said.

"He says this one's for you," Zeus said, and he handed the sword to Ron.

Ron looked at the sword, his eyes wide. "This is a pretty nice one."

"You'll need a scabbard," Hera said, handing him a leather belt with a long, deep pocket on the side. She was wearing one herself and had already placed her sword in it. "See?"

Ron put on the belt. It hung loosely around his waist. Then he slipped the sword into the scabbard. The weapon was almost as tall as him.

"How do I look?" Ron asked.

"Like a hero in training," Hera replied, smiling. "Not bad."

Ron straightened up a little bit. "Come on. Let's go to the kitchens and get some food for our trip. The edge of the kingdom is a few hours away if we walk."

In the kitchens they filled their packs with figs, cheese, bread, and dried fish. Then they headed outside to begin their journey. King Iobates was waiting for them by Pegasus.

"Ah, there you are," he said. "So do you think you'll reach the outskirts by nightfall?"

"Definitely," Ron said. "We should be there before the monster shows up."

"Excellent," the king said, and Zeus noticed a strange gleam in his eye. "Good luck, Nephew!"

They headed off. Ron rode on top of Pegasus, who walked slowly so the others could keep up. Ron sat up straight in the saddle when he rode.

"So I guess you're not afraid of horses, then?" Zeus asked him.

Ron smiled and patted Pegasus's head. "Not this one, for some reason."

They walked for hours and didn't stop until they reached a small village dotted with humble huts. There wasn't a person in sight. Then Zeus saw a door slowly creak open, and a face peeked out.

A man ran out. "It's a boy on a winged horse! He's come to save us!" the man yelled.

The villagers ran out of their tiny cottages and surrounded Ron. Nobody seemed to even notice the Olympians.

"Ahem, excuse me!" Hera called out loudly. But the crowd was too busy petting the horse and cheering for Ron.

"I hardly blame them," Athena said. "I mean, look at him and look at us!"

Zeus gazed up at Ron. His white toga gleamed in the fading afternoon sunlight. Up on the horse, he didn't look so short. His golden curls waved gently in the breeze.

Then Zeus looked around at the Olympians. King Iobates had been right. They did look a bit, well, raggedy. It was no wonder the villagers were ignoring them.

"Come on," Zeus said. "Let's find a place where we can make a plan to defeat the Chimera." As they broke away, Ron didn't even seem to notice the group was leaving as he soaked up the attention from the adoring crowd.

They walked until they came to a large, flat rock just outside the village. Hephaestus and Hestia sat down on it.

"My mouth is as parched and dry as the flaming fields of the Underworld," Hades said. "Is there any water around here?"

Zeus nodded. "I think there's a stream over there. I'm going to grab something to drink." He held out his water horn.

"I'll go with you," Hades offered.

"We can put out some food," Demeter said. "It's been a long time since we ate anything."

The sun was just starting to set as the boys headed for the stream. As they got closer, Hades stopped suddenly and tapped Zeus's arm.

"Do you hear that?" Hades asked.

Deep voices floated to them from across the stream, along with the sound of feet marching on grass—big feet. Instinct took over, and Zeus and Hades ducked behind a bush.

"I'm confused," one deep voice said. "Do we take all of the kids?"

"I keep telling you, not all!" said another deep voice. "King Iobates said to leave the littlest blond one, the one on the flying horse.

77

But the rest we can capture and bring back to King Cronus."

"Cronies!" Hades whispered.

Zeus put a finger over his lips and peeked out. Two Cronies stood across the stream. They might have been only half-giants, but they were taller than any human. One had a thick mat of black hair, and the other was bald and wore one gold earring. They each wore a loincloth and carried a long, spiked staff.

King Iobates must have told them about the Olympians, Zeus realized. It figured that guy would be a fan of King Cronus!

"Let's go get 'em!" said the black-haired Crony.

"Just remember, don't hurt them too much," said the bald one. "King Cronus wants them alive so that he can gobble them up himself."

A rush of anger swept through Zeus again.

He jumped out from behind the bush.

"Nobody is hurting us!" he yelled, and he held Bolt up high. "Bolt, do it!"

A sizzling lightning bolt of electricity shot from Bolt and hit the tree branch right above the Cronies. The branch fell on top of them and pinned them to the ground.

Hades grabbed Zeus's sleeve. "Come on. We need to go warn the others!"

They ran back to the rest of the Olympians.

"Cronies!" Hades yelled. "We've got to get out of here."

"But shouldn't we wait for Ron? I'm sure he will catch up to us soon," Hera pointed out. "How many are there? We should stand and fight."

"Uh, looks like it's two of them," Poseidon said, pointing.

The two angry Cronies were marching toward them.

"Olympians! Magical weapons!" Zeus cried.

The Olympians quickly formed a line and started to hold up their magical weapons. But before they could combine their powers, a loud roar filled the air. It sounded almost like thunder.

The two Cronies stopped in their tracks.

"Do . . . do you see that?" said Crony One, his voice quivering.

The other Crony didn't even answer. They both turned around and ran away as fast as they could.

The Olympians slowly turned to look behind them.

A creature as big as a house stood in the field, roaring loudly. The body was half lion, half goat—with big muscles, golden fur and a goat's head coming off the back of its body. It had a fierce-looking tail that was long and green, and ended in a head with red eyes and sharp teeth—just like a snake. Its main head looked just like a lion—big, bold, and with very scary rows of sharp teeth—and it was looking right at the Olympians!

"It's the Chimera!" Zeus yelled.

CHAPTER NINE

Ron to the Rescue

So what's our plan?" Poseidon asked.

"Quick! Let's power up our weapons!" Zeus yelled.

"You don't need to. Just let me turn the Chimera into stone!" cried Athena.

She ran forward, untying her cloak. Then she pulled it open to reveal the shining aegis underneath, emblazoned with the terrifying image of Medusa's head.

"Hey!" she called up to the Chimera. "Take a look at this!"

The monster swatted at Athena with a huge paw. The Olympian went flying across the field and landed in a heap.

"Athena!" Demeter ran to her fallen friend.

"Weapons, now!" Zeus yelled. "Bolt, large!"

The dagger instantly grew into a giant lightning bolt, and Zeus raised it. Poseidon extended his trident. Hades lifted up his helmet. Hestia held up her torch. Hera added her peacock feather, and Hephaestus joined in with his cane.

The magic objects sizzled with energy. The Chimera roared loudly and sprang toward them.

Boom! A burst of energy exploded from the weapons in a brilliant white blast. The Chimera shrieked and fell backward.

All six magical objects were glowing now, even Hera's feather.

"Surround the monster!" Zeus commanded.

The Olympians started to run. But Hephaestus wasn't moving. His supercharged cane was moving back and forth wildly in his hand.

"Whoa!" Hephaestus cried.

The cane flew out of his hands! Then it soared across the field like an arrow. One by one it knocked the items out of the Olympians' hands! Bolt flew from Zeus's grasp. Hades dropped his helmet. Hestia lost her torch. Poseidon's trident went flying. Only Hera held on to her feather.

"Can't you control that thing?" she yelled at Hephaestus.

The Chimera was back on its feet—and it was angry. Zeus scrambled to pick up Bolt. But the supercharge had faded.

The Chimera lunged toward the Olympians, roaring loudly.

"Bolt!" Zeus cried, and he hurled the weapon.

Bolt hit the beast with sizzling energy. It stopped the Chimera for a moment, but the monster shook off the attack as though it had been nothing.

"Bath time!" Poseidon cried. He pounded his trident into the ground, and a powerful spring of water shot up. It hit the Chimera right in the lion's face, but the force wasn't strong enough to take down the beast.

Hestia, meanwhile, was running circles around the Chimera with her lit torch. As she ran, a ring of fire sprang up around the monster. The flames leaped higher and higher.

"Nice job, Sis!" Hades told her, slapping her hand when she returned.

But the Chimera's roar was louder than the roaring flames. The beast started to pat down the flames with its huge, padded paws.

"We can't stop it!" Hephaestus said. "We should get out of here!"

"Let me try again!" Athena ran up to the other Olympians, her cloak flapping out behind her. Demeter was at her heels.

"Athena, it's too dangerous!" Zeus warned.

Athena got right underneath the Chimera. "Come on, scaredy-cat, look!"

There was a flash of green as the beast's serpent tail lashed out at Athena, who cried out and stumbled backward.

"It bit me!" she shrieked. Then she fell to her knees.

"Leave her alone!" The voice came from overhead. Zeus looked up. Ron, flying on Pegasus, was heading toward the Chimera.

The monster rose on its two hind legs and swatted at the flying horse. Ron steered the horse toward the ground quickly. He reached down, grabbed Athena, and pulled her onto Pegasus.

They all flew back toward the other

Olympians. The horse landed, and Hera and Hades gently lifted Athena to the ground. Athena's eyes were closed, and her skin was a pale green.

Then Ron took off again. "Let me finish this," he said.

"Ron, you can't do this by yourself!" Zeus told him.

But Ron flew straight toward the snarling, thrashing beast, and across its back. Ron took out his sword.

Before he could swing, the goat's head chomped on to Ron's toga! It pulled him off Pegasus's back and sent Ron flying.

Pegasus whinnied. Angry, the horse circled the Chimera and then flew toward it.

The Chimera's lion head roared as the beast reached for Pegasus with its claws.

Zeus zapped the Chimera again with Bolt.

That stopped the monster for a second, and Pegasus flew out of danger.

"We've got to go!" Hera urged. "Athena needs help!"

Zeus's mind was racing. If they ran, the Chimera would chase them. Even if they somehow outran the beast, it would only attack the village. They had to stay and fight. But how could they defeat it?

"Look!" Demeter cried, pointing.

Hermes was flying right toward the Chimera, his wand extended in front of him.

"Time for some magic!" he called out.

CHAPTER TEN

Stars in the Sky

ermes's wand glowed with blue light. He aimed the wand at the Chimera, and when the blue light hit, the Chimera let out a mighty roar. But that didn't slow the beast down.

Zeus's heart sank. Bolt's zap hadn't stopped the Chimera. So the wand would surely fail too.

Then something strange happened. The Chimera's body started to glimmer and shimmer.

The Olympians watched, wide-eyed, as the monster seemed to dissolve in front of their eyes into glittering dots.

Then Hermes pointed his wand up at the sky. The first stars were shining in the deep-blue heavens. The shimmering body of the Chimera flew up into the air, and the glittering dots scattered across the sky, joining the other stars.

"He did it!" Poseidon cheered. "He defeated the monster!"

Hermes flew down to the other Olympians. Ron, whose white tunic was now stained with dirt and grass, walked up, leading Pegasus.

"How did you do that?" Zeus asked Hermes.

"I'm not exactly sure," the boy admitted. "The powers of the wand seem to be connected to the sky. I can turn things into birds and stars and clouds. But I also used it to get rid of a bad cold once."

"You mean you can heal with that thing?" Hera asked. "Then get over here and help Athena!"

Hera and Hades were cradling Athena. Hermes flew over to them, with the others running behind.

"She got bitten by the snake part of the Chimera," Hades reported.

Athena's skin was still green, and she was letting out little coughs every few seconds.

"Whoa," Hermes said. "Looks serious. But I guess I can try."

He waved his wand over Athena. Nothing glowed or shimmered this time. Everyone held their breath.

I hope this works, Zeus thought.

Athena's eyes slowly began to flutter. The green in her skin began to fade.

"It's working!" Hades cried.

Athena slowly sat up. "What happened?"

"The Chimera's snake tail bit you," Hera told

her. "But Hermes came back and turned the Chimera into stars. And then he used the wand to heal you."

Athena smiled weakly. "Thank you."

"That's not all that happened," Zeus said. "Before Hermes got here, Ron and Pegasus flew into the fight. He got you out of the way before the Chimera could hurt you any more."

Athena turned to Ron. "Thank you, too, then," she said. "That sounds very brave for somebody who's afraid of everything."

Ron's cheeks turned pink. "Well, I was in the village, and I heard the big explosion."

"That was us charging up our weapons," Zeus informed him.

"I knew you were in trouble, so I jumped on Pegasus and flew in," Ron continued. "When I saw Athena lying there, I didn't think to be afraid. I just wanted to help."

"Just like a true hero," Demeter said with a smile, and Ron blushed again.

"Your uncle will be proud of you," Hestia said.

"Even though he's horrible," Hera reminded everyone. "He sent the Cronies after us!"

Ron looked shocked. "No way! He did that?"

Zeus nodded. "Yes, right before the Chimera attacked."

Ron frowned. "I don't think I'm going back there, then," he said. "Pegasus and I can fly anywhere we want. Right, Pegasus?"

He patted the horse's nose, and Pegasus whinnied.

"That's right, young man. The world is your clam. Or maybe it's your oyster?"

The voice was coming from a shimmering cloud. Then a figure appeared inside the cloud—a woman with long, black hair and glasses.

"Pythia!" Zeus cried.

Athena jumped to her feet as the Oracle of Delphi appeared in the middle of the Olympians.

"Pythia, where have you been?" Hera asked.

"Well, dear, I did not visit sooner because I knew the only way Hermes would join you would be if he met you himself," she said. She straightened her glasses. "I see that worked out."

Zeus smiled. "Yeah, it worked out pretty well."

"So what's our next quest?" Poseidon asked.

"It's not just your next quest—it's your last quest!" Pythia announced. "You have only one more Olympian to find."

"Who is she?" Hera asked.

"Where will we find him?" asked Hephaestus.

"The future is foggy, as always," Pythia said, squinting through her glasses. "I think you need to go to . . . the Land of Apes."

"What's an ape?" Hades asked.

"I don't think we have any in Greece," Athena said.

"Wait . . . wait . . . ," Pythia continued. "Maybe it's the Land of Grapes. That's it! The Land of Grapes!"

"That makes more sense," Hephaestus grumbled.

"Well, I'm not going anywhere until we find Apollo, Artemis, Aphrodite, and Ares," Zeus said.

"And you shouldn't," Pythia said. "For this journey, you will need all of your powers combined. You will face your most dangerous monster ever."

"More dangerous than a Chimera? Flipping fish sticks!" exclaimed Poseidon.

"What kind of monster is it, exactly?" Hera wanted to know.

Pythia squinted again. "I can see it. It's very . . . very . . . Oh my!"

The cloud began to shimmer, and Pythia started to disappear.

"No! Wait! Tell us more!" Zeus yelled.

But Pythia was gone.

"So we've got to go fight another monster?" Demeter asked.

"Can't we rest first?" Hades asked.

Zeus looked up at the sky filled with shimmering stars. "Of course," he said.

"Let's get to the village," Ron suggested. "The villagers are really nice. I'm sure they'll put us up for the night."

"Last one there is a loser!" shouted Hermes, and he swiftly flew toward the village.

Zeus shook his head. "He's annoying, but I'm sure glad we found him."

"And now we only have one more Olympian to find," said Hera.

"And then I guess we fight King Cronus once and for all," added Poseidon.

Zeus thought about this. Poseidon was right. Once they found the Olympian, it would be time for the big battle. Zeus had never been sure that they could do it. But with each Olympian they met, they got stronger.

Zeus couldn't believe there was just one Olympian left to find! But he knew that first they needed to reunite with the other four Olympians so that they could embark on this last quest together.

He grinned and broke into a run.

"We're right behind you, Hermes!" he yelled.

Join Zeus and his friends
as they set off on the
adventure of a lifetime.

Now Available:

#1 Zeus and the Thunderbolt of Doom

#2 Poseidon and the Sea of Fury

#3 Hades and the Helm of Darkness

#4 Hyperion and the Great Balls of Fire

#5 Typhon and the Winds of Destruction

#6 Apollo and the Battle of the Birds

#7 Ares and the Spear of Fear

#8 Cronus and the Threads of Dread

#9 Crius and the Night of Fright

#10 Hephaestus and the Island of Terror

#11 Uranus and the Bubbles of Trouble

#12 Perseus and the Monstrous Medusa

EBOOK EDITIONS ALSO AVAILABLE
From Aladdin • simonandschuster.com/kids

Looking for another great book?
Find it
IN THE MIDDLE.

Fun, fantastic books for kids
in the in-be**TWEEN** age.

IntheMiddleBooks.com

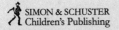